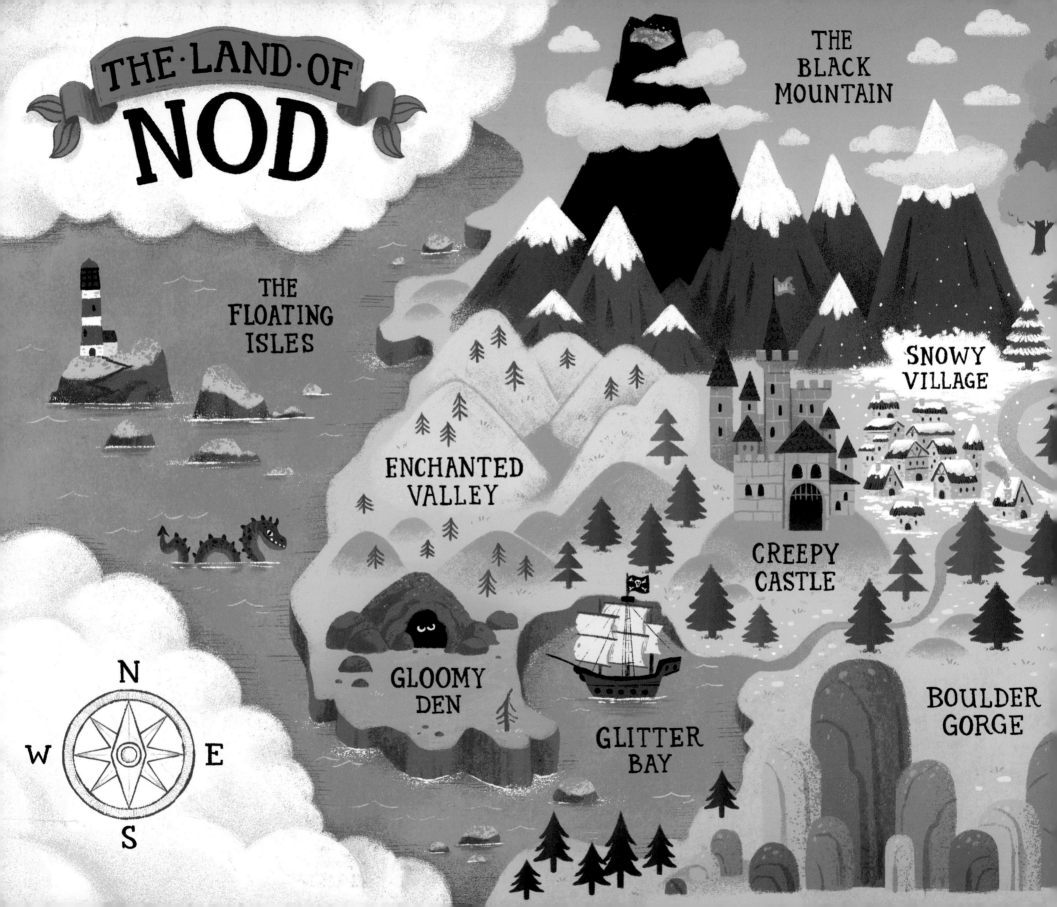

For Finn, the merbaby
R.F.

For Jules, just keep swimming
C.C.

LADYBIRD BOOKS

Ladybird Books is part of the Penguin Random House group of companies
whose addresses can be found at global.penguinrandomhouse.com.

www.penguin.co.uk   www.puffin.co.uk   www.ladybird.co.uk

Penguin
Random House
UK

First published 2019
001
Written by Rhiannon Fielding. Text copyright © Ladybird Books Ltd, 2019
Illustrations copyright © Chris Chatterton, 2019
Moral rights asserted
Printed in China
A CIP catalogue record for this book is available from the British Library
ISBN: 978–0–241–37267–8
All correspondence to:
Ladybird Books, Penguin Random House Children's
80 Strand, London WC2R 0RL

TEN MINUTES TO BED

Little Mermaid

Rhiannon Fielding • Chris Chatterton

Deep below the ocean waves,
among the wild sea-flowers,
a palace stood, with shells for walls,
and shining pearls for towers.

In the kingdom of the **merpeople**,
merchildren whizzed around!
With **ten minutes** to bedtime, though . . .

someone **could not** be found.

Splash was with the dolphins!

They were

d
 i
  v
   i
    n
     g,

playing,

leaping!

"Nine minutes!"
came her grandpa's call . . .
Splash **did not** feel like sleeping.

She wished she wasn't quite so small;
she wanted to be **brave**.
So with **eight minutes** to bedtime

Splash dived deep beneath a wave.

The soft and sandy ocean floor
was **bumping** with a **beat**.

"Seven minutes!" called the crabs,
as they **clacked** their claws and feet.

Through the water swiftly swam
a shoal of rainbow fish.

"Six minutes to bed!" they said as one –
"Come with us if you wish!"

As Splash's little tail grew tired, the fish all swam away.

"Five minutes!"
croaked a turtle,

as they bobbed
around the bay.

Suddenly, a **shadow** slunk

across the ocean floor.

Four minutes to bed,
and up Splash leapt!

The shark opened its jaw . . .

But with a plop! Splash landed on a golden island beach.
"Three minutes," laughed a passing whale.

"Hop on if you can reach!"

Zooming through the ocean
as the spray fell down in showers,

with two minutes to bedtime
Splash could see the palace towers!

"Thank you," said the mermaid
as she kissed her whale friend's head.
"One minute!" called her grandpa's voice . . .

then Splash
swam into bed.

This daring **little mermaid** has a secret now to keep: **adventure** is all very well . . .

but mermaids
need their sleep!

THE·LAND·OF
NOD

THE
BLACK
MOUNTAIN

THE
FLOATING
ISLES

SNOWY
VILLAGE

ENCHANTED
VALLEY

CREEPY
CASTLE

GLOOMY
DEN

BOULDER
GORGE

GLITTER
BAY

THE
ANCIENT FOREST

OUTER
SPACE

EMERALD
GLEN

DEADLY
CREEK

GIANTS' TOWN

THE
STINKY
SWAMPS

GOLDEN
COVE

RICKETY
BRIDGE

Look out for more bedtime adventures in

THE·LAND·OF
NOD

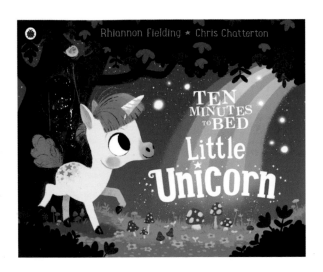